P9-DNT-880

SEP - - 2016

DRAGON MASTERS
SECRET OF THE WATER DRAGON

BY
TRACEY WEST

ILLUSTRATED BY
GRAHAM HOWELLS

BRANCHES
SCHOLASTIC INC.

ST. THOMAS PUBLIC LIBRARY

DRAGON MASTERS

Read All the Books

TABLE OF CONTENTS

FOR BOLLIE DUNGAN,

because every girl detective needs a smarter, funnier sidekick. —TW

Special thanks to Damien Jones for his artistic contributions to this book.

If you purchased this book without a cover, you should be aware that this book is stolen property. It was reported as "unsold and destroyed" to the publisher, and neither the author nor the publisher has received any payment for this "stripped book."

No part of this publication may be reproduced, stored in a retrieval system, or transmitted in any form or by any means, electronic, mechanical, photocopying, recording, or otherwise, without written permission of the publisher. For information regarding permission, write to Scholastic Inc., Attention: Permissions Department, 557 Broadway, New York, NY 10012.

Library of Congress Cataloging-in-Publication Data
West, Tracey, 1965-
Secret of the water dragon / by Tracey West ; illustrated by Graham Howells.
pages cm. — (Dragon masters ; 3)
Summary: When Drake discovers that his friend and fellow Dragon Master, Bo, is trying to steal the Dragon Stone, he wonders if the dark wizard might be behind it, and he must try to find a way to protect the stone while keeping Bo's family out of danger.
ISBN 0-545-64628-6 (pbk.) — ISBN 0-545-64630-8 (hardcover) — ISBN 0-545-64635-9 (ebook)
[1. Dragons—Fiction. 2. Wizards—Fiction. 3.Magic—Fiction. 4. Stealing—Fiction.]
I. Howells, Graham, illustrator.
II. Title.
PZ7.W51937Sct 2015
[Fic]—dc23
2014017064

ISBN 978-0-545-64630-7 (hardcover) / ISBN 978-0-545-64628-4 (paperback)

Text copyright © 2015 by Tracey West.
Interior illustrations copyright © 2015 by Scholastic Inc.

All rights reserved. Published by Scholastic Inc.
SCHOLASTIC, BRANCHES, and associated logos are trademarks and/or registered trademarks of Scholastic Inc.

10 9 8 7 6 5 4   15 16 17 18 19 20/0

Printed in China   38
First printing, March 2015
Illustrated by Graham Howells
Edited by Katie Carella
Book design by Jessica Meltzer

SADDLE UP!

"Steady now," warned Griffith, the king's wizard. "We have never tried putting a saddle on a dragon before. I am not sure how she will like it."

Griffith and the Dragon Masters were in the Training Room, hidden beneath King Roland's castle. A magical stone called the Dragon Stone had chosen Drake, Bo, Rori, and Ana to work with dragons. Griffith was their teacher. The Dragon Masters stood around a big dragon with shiny blue scales.

"Bo, bring the buckle under Shu's belly," Griffith said. "Now tighten the buckle. Good!"

Drake watched his friend Bo put the saddle on Shu. She was a Water Dragon, so she was usually very calm. Shu stood still as Bo pulled the buckle tightly.

"Good job, Shu," Bo said, patting her neck.

"Now can I put a saddle on Vulcan?" asked Rori.

"And can we please ride our dragons today, Griffith?" asked Ana.

"King Roland's crafters are making a saddle for each dragon," answered Griffith. "The other saddles will be ready tomorrow."

"Will there be a saddle for Worm?" asked Drake. He looked over at his dragon. Worm was an Earth Dragon. He had a long body, like a snake. He had no legs, and tiny wings. Worm couldn't fly like the other dragons could.

"Yes. Worm has a very special power. He can take you from one place to another in the blink of an eye," Griffith said. "A saddle is a good idea for any type of travel."

Drake nodded.

"It is time for dinner," said Griffith. "Please put away your dragons and head to the dining room."

"Well, I hope *I* get to test Vulcan's saddle *first* tomorrow," Rori said. "Vulcan and I didn't get to do anything fun today."

She marched off toward the Dragon Caves. Her dragon, Vulcan, stomped after her. He was a Fire Dragon with red scales.

Ana followed Rori. She skipped along. Her dragon, Kepri, moved like a graceful dancer beside her. Kepri was a Sun Dragon with a slim body and white scales.

Drake helped Bo take off Shu's saddle. They put their dragons in their caves. Then they took the stairs to the dining room in the tower. After dinner, the boys went to their room.

Drake touched his Dragon Stone as they walked. Each of the Dragon Masters wore a piece of the stone. It let them connect with their dragons.

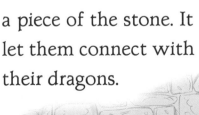

"Bo," Drake said, "do you think Worm can go anywhere in the world?"

"I think so," Bo said. "He has very strong powers."

Bo opened the door. Then he froze. Drake bumped into him.

"Bo, what's wrong?" Drake asked. His friend was staring at his bed. His face looked pale.

Drake followed his gaze. A black feather lay on Bo's pillow.

CHAPTER 2

THE BLACK FEATHER

"hat's strange," Drake said. "We must've left the window open."

Bo sat down on the bed and picked up the feather. He looked worried.

"Bo, it's just a feather," Drake said. "What's wrong?"

"Nothing. I am fine," Bo said.

But Drake didn't believe him.

Bo was quiet as the boys climbed into bed. He rolled over and faced the wall.

Drake could tell that something was bothering Bo. *But why would a feather upset him?*

Drake drifted off to sleep, thinking about his friend: *I hope he's okay.*

When Drake woke up in the morning, Bo was sitting up in bed. He was wide-awake.

"Wow! Have you been up a long time?" said Drake.

Bo shrugged. "Um . . . I'm just excited to ride Shu today."

But Drake did not hear excitement in Bo's voice.

The boys headed down to breakfast. Ana and Rori were already eating.

"It's about time you two sleepyheads got here," said Rori.

"I can't wait to get outside!" said Ana. "Last night, Kepri sent a picture to my mind. We were flying in the sky. She sends me lots of pictures since we made our connection."

Drake nodded. He and Worm had formed a strong connection, too. He could hear Worm in his head. His Dragon Stone glowed green every time it happened. But this hadn't happened for Bo and Shu yet. Or for Rori and Vulcan.

"I'm sure we will go right outside. Where is Griffith?" Bo asked, looking around.

Rori shrugged. "He's probably getting the saddles ready. Hurry up and eat!"

Drake was excited to test out Worm's saddle. He wolfed down his breakfast.

"Let's go!" Rori said as soon as Drake was done. Drake got up and put an apple in his pocket to give Worm. Ana grabbed Bo's arm and pulled him off his seat. As they left, Drake looked back. Bo had hardly eaten breakfast.

Downstairs, they found Griffith waiting for them in the Training Room. He had a serious look on his face.

"What's wrong?" Ana asked.

"Somebody tried to steal the Dragon Stone!" he said.

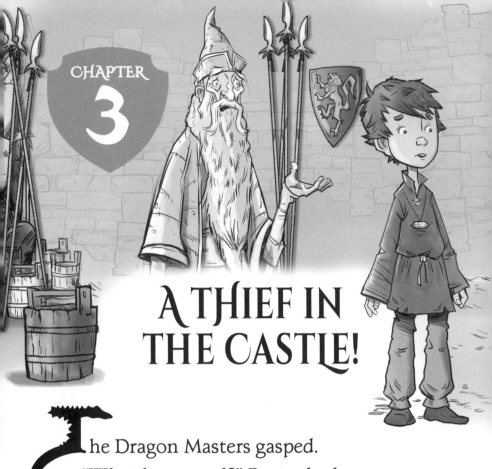

CHAPTER 3

A THIEF IN THE CASTLE!

The Dragon Masters gasped.

"What happened?" Rori asked.

"I always protect the stone with magic charms," Griffith explained. "These charms cannot be seen. But they form an invisible net around the box that holds the Dragon Stone. And they can only be broken with a magic spell."

"So how do you know someone tried to steal the stone?" asked Drake.

"This morning, I found that something had upset the magic of the charms. They were not broken, but I could tell that someone had tried to break them," Griffith answered.

Ana gripped the stone around her neck. "If somebody steals the main Dragon Stone would our smaller stones lose their powers?"

"No," the wizard replied. "But someone could use the main stone to control the dragons. Or even to form a dragon army."

"Isn't that what King Roland is doing?" asked Drake.

"King Roland wants to use the dragons for good. I have known King Roland since he was a boy. He is a good man at heart. And as long as the stone is in my care, I can keep it safe. Safe from people like Maldred . . ." He shuddered.

The Dragon Masters looked at one another.

"You mean Maldred the dark wizard? Is he the one who tried to steal the Dragon Stone last night?" Drake asked.

The Dragon Masters all knew that Maldred had tried to get to their dragons before. They had never seen Maldred. But already, his dark magic had caused a lot of trouble.

Griffith shook his head. "No," he said. "Maldred would not have been so careless. He would have broken the charms using a spell. Our thief clearly did not know about the charms."

Drake glanced at Bo. His friend kept looking nervously over his shoulder.

"To protect the Dragon Stone, I must find a better hiding place for it," Griffith continued. "I will leave the castle right away to look for one."

"So there's no riding practice today?" Ana asked. She looked at the finished saddles.

"You may go outside and have a free day. But the dragons must stay inside," he said. Then he hurried out of the room.

"What do we do now?" Rori asked.

"Well, we can still spend the day with our dragons," Drake replied. "We can hang out with them in the caves."

"I — I must go," Bo said. "There is something I must take care of."

"What —" Drake began. But Bo was already rushing off.

"*He's* acting strange," Rori said, with her hands on her hips.

Ana nodded. "Yes, he seems quieter than usual today."

"I think something is worrying him," Drake said, remembering the black feather.

"Maybe he's worried about the Dragon Stone," said Rori.

As they headed to the Dragon Caves, Drake kept looking behind him.

Was the thief still in the castle?

THE WIZARD'S TRAP

Worm looked up as soon as Drake reached his cave. Drake took the apple from breakfast out of his pocket.

"Good morning, Worm," Drake said, holding out the treat. The dragon craned his long neck. He grabbed the apple in his teeth and ate it in one gulp.

Drake sat down on the cold floor of the cave.

"Somebody tried to steal the Dragon Stone last night," Drake said. "Griffith is finding a new hiding place for the stone. So we have a free day."

Rori and Ana walked up to Worm's cave.

"Come on, Drake! We're going outside," Rori said.

"Yeah, we don't want to be stuck in here all day," said Ana. "Coming?"

Drake shook his head. "No, thanks. I'm going to stay with Worm."

Rori shrugged. "Have fun in the dark! We'll be outside!"

The girls walked away. Drake started to tell Worm a story about when he lived back on the onion farm. Suddenly, Worm's neck jerked up. His eyes glowed green.

"What is it, Worm?" asked Drake.

Drake's Dragon Stone glowed, too. Then he heard Worm's voice in his head.

Bo.

"What about Bo? Is he in trouble?" Drake asked.

Worm nodded.

Drake jumped up. He ran out of the caves and through the Training Room. He was on the way to their room when he heard noises coming from inside Griffith's workshop. But he knew Griffith had left the castle.

Is someone in there? Drake wondered.

The door was open a crack. He peeked inside.

Bo was in Griffith's workshop — with one hand on the box that held the Dragon Stone!

Drake held back a gasp. Bo was reading aloud from a book. The words sounded magical, like something a wizard would say. *The charms protecting the stone could only be broken by a magic spell*, he remembered. Then a terrible thought hit him: *Is Bo trying to steal the Dragon Stone?!*

Drake pushed open the door. He had to stop Bo!

Suddenly, sparks shot out from the corner of the room. They hit the book Bo was holding and it fell to the ground. Griffith stepped out of the shadows. His finger was pointed at Bo.

"Stop, thief!"

BO'S STORY

Bo's hands were shaking. He looked up at Griffith.

Drake stood frozen in the doorway.

"Come in, Drake," Griffith said. Drake obeyed. The wizard's eyes stayed on Bo. "This is very serious. I set this trap because I thought someone *inside* the castle had tried to steal the stone last night. I said I was leaving the castle, but then I hid in here. I had to see if the thief would come back. And he did — *you* did."

Bo looked down at his shoes. "I am sorry," he said softly.

"Bo, tell me why you would do such a thing," Griffith said.

"I . . ." Bo looked up. "I cannot say."

"Please, Bo!" Drake blurted out. "I *know* you! You wouldn't steal anything. You have to explain."

Griffith looked into Bo's eyes. "We can help you, Bo," he said. "But you must tell us why you tried to steal the stone."

Bo sighed. "It began when King Roland's soldiers came to my kingdom. They went to see Emperor Song."

"What did they want?" Drake asked.

"They wanted *me*," Bo replied. "The soldiers told the emperor that King Roland wanted me for an important project. At first, Emperor Song did not agree to send me off. He was worried that I would not be safe. But my parents said it would be an honor to our kingdom. So he agreed."

Drake nodded. "Emperor Song sounds very kind."

"He is — or at least, he used to be," Bo said. "Last night, I found a black feather on my pillow. There was a note with it that I did not show Drake."

He took a piece of paper from his pocket and gave it to Griffith.

"It says —" His voice choked. "It says that Emperor Song has put my family in prison. To save them, I must steal the Dragon Stone and bring it to him right away. And I must not tell anyone." His eyes filled with tears.

Griffith put a hand on his shoulder. "I understand."

"But you said he was a kind emperor, Bo," Drake said. "Why would he do this?"

"I do not know," Bo replied. "I fear that some evil has come over him."

"I fear you are right," said the wizard. "And we must help your emperor. But first, we have a problem closer to home. The black feather is a symbol of the Raven Guard."

Bo nodded. "Yes. You have heard of them?"

"I have heard stories," Griffith said. "The Raven Guard is a group of skilled fighters who serve the emperor. They are very dangerous."

Drake turned pale. "So if the feather is in the castle . . ."

"Then one of the Raven Guards is here, too!" said Bo.

CHAPTER 6

THE RAVEN GUARD

W hat do you know about the Raven Guards, Bo?" asked Griffith.

"They dress all in black," said Bo. "They can move silently without being seen."

"They *must* be sneaky," said Drake. "How else could one of them get that feather on your pillow?"

Bo nodded. "They are very skilled at spying."

Just then, Drake's Dragon Stone felt warm on his skin. He looked down. It was glowing! Then he heard Worm's voice inside his head.

Danger outside!

"Rori and Ana!" Drake cried. "They went outside by themselves!"

Griffith frowned. "We must find them." He stomped into the hallway and yelled to the guard by the Training Room door. "Simon, please watch my workshop! Make sure no one enters!"

Simon grunted in reply, and the three of them rushed out of the workshop. They raced through the long tunnel that led to the Valley of Clouds.

When they got outside, Rori and Ana ran up to them. They both started talking quickly.

"The thief was here! He was dressed in black!" cried Ana.

"He had a red crystal! And he shone it in our eyes," Rori said.

"Then he started asking us stuff! And we gave him answers!" Ana said. "Somehow he *made* us tell the truth, even though we did not want to. I think the crystal was —"

"Magic!" Rori added. "And then he was gone! He moved so fast!"

"He is a skilled and dangerous spy," said Griffith. "The red crystal he used sounds like dark magic. Now, tell me: What questions did he ask?"

"He wanted to know where the Dragon Stone was," Ana replied. "And if it was guarded by anything."

"*Ana* told him about the magic charms!" Rori said.

"And *you* told him Griffith had left the castle," Ana said.

"Wait a minute, Griffith. What are you doing here?" Rori asked.

"Never mind that," Griffith said. "I am here now. And the spy may be on his way to steal the Dragon Stone. We must get to my workshop. Hurry!"

They all raced back through the tunnel. Drake's heart pounded.

When they got to Griffith's office, Simon the guard was conked out on the floor! And the workshop door was wide open!

THE CHASE

Griffith ran to the box that held the Dragon Stone. He opened the lid.

"The Dragon Stone is gone!" he cried.

"The Raven Guard must have come right for it," Bo said.

"Raven Guard? What do you mean, Bo?" Rori asked, her green eyes flashing. "What is going on?"

Bo told Rori and Ana everything — about the feather, the Raven Guard, and Emperor Song.

"So *you* tried to steal the stone last night?" Ana asked Bo. "And that spy came from *your* kingdom?"

Bo nodded.

"Now, Dragon Masters, we must act quickly," Griffith said. He picked up a small box and opened it. A green feather floated in the air.

"I put a magic Finding Charm on the Dragon Stone," he said. "This feather will lead us to it. But we must hurry!"

Bo nodded. "The Raven Guard moves swiftly."

"We will use our two fastest dragons — and their new saddles," Griffith said. "Rori, you and I will take Vulcan. Ana, you and Drake take Kepri."

"What about me?" asked Bo.

"You will stay here," said Griffith. "Make sure Simon is all right."

Bo nodded. "Yes, Griffith."

Drake and the others raced to the dragon caves. He and Ana quickly saddled Kepri and climbed on her back. Rori and Griffith climbed on Vulcan.

"Feather, find the stone!" Griffith commanded. The feather zipped toward the tunnels.

Vulcan took off after the feather like a shot. Kepri was on his tail. When the feather left the tunnels, the dragons took to the air. They flew across the Valley of Clouds.

Drake looked down. His stomach flipped.
"We're so high up!" he yelled to Ana.
"Isn't it amazing?!" she yelled back.
Wind brushed Drake's cheeks as the dragons
flew across the Valley of Clouds. They flew
over the hills, to the deep, wide forest beyond.

Drake kept his eyes on the feather. Up ahead, he could see something moving across the treetops: the Raven Guard! The small, black figure moved like the wind from one tree to the next.

Griffith saw him, too. So he plucked the Finding Feather from the air. He pointed down. Vulcan dove through the trees.

Drake's stomach flipped as Kepri followed. The two dragons glided side by side over the treetops.

"We're catching up to him!" Ana shouted, her dark eyes gleaming.

Vulcan was closest to the guard. The dragon opened his mouth wide.

"No, Vulcan!" Griffith yelled. "No fire! It's too dangerous! Ana, pull ahead with Kepri! Block the guard, and I will use a spell on him!"

"Faster, Kepri!" Ana told her dragon. "Get in front of that guy!"

Kepri picked up speed. She flew past the quickly moving guard. Then she turned around, blocking his path.

Drake saw that the guard wore all black. Only his eyes were showing. The guard reached into a pocket. He pulled out a handful of glittering, red dust.

Red: the color of
dark magic. The color
of the crystal that the
guard had used to make
Rori and Ana answer him.

The same color as
the ball of light that
Maldred had sent into
the castle weeks ago.

*The dust must be
dark magic, too*, Drake
guessed.

"Ana! Turn Kepri back NOW!" he yelled.
"It's dark magic!"

Dark magic makes
Sun Dragons sick.
Drake knew they
had to get Kepri
away from here
before the red
dust came near her.

Ana quickly steered Kepri away from the guard. Drake looked back at Griffith. The wizard's finger was pointed at the guard. He was starting to say a spell.

That's when Drake noticed the bag in the guard's hand.

The Dragon Stone must be in that bag! he thought.

"Rori! Grab the bag!" Drake yelled.

The guard quickly sprinkled red powder on himself.

Then everything happened at once.

Vulcan charged at the guard from behind. Rori reached out and yanked the bag out of the guard's hand. His eyes widened.

The red dust sparkled. Vulcan roared loudly. He blasted a stream of fire as the guard disappeared.

"Vulcan, no!" Rori cried.

The treetops burst into flame!

SHU TO THE RESCUE

"Higher! Fly above the smoke!" Griffith yelled over the roar of the flames.

Vulcan and Kepri flew above the fire. Then a blue streak darted out in front of them.

It was Bo, riding his dragon! *But Bo isn't supposed to be outside!* thought Drake.

A powerful wave of water streamed out of Shu's mouth. The fire sizzled, then went out.

"I am sorry I did not stay behind," Bo told Griffith. "But when I looked outside and saw the smoke, Shu and I just had to help."

"You did well," Griffith told him. Bo smiled proudly.

"Rori, do you have the stone?" Griffith called out.

Rori opened the bag. The big, green Dragon Stone glittered inside.

"Got it!" she yelled back.

"Then to the castle! Hurry!" the wizard ordered.

They quickly flew back to the caves and climbed off the dragons.

"Bo, that was awesome!" said Ana. "Shu did a great job putting out that fire. And, Rori, you did a great job getting back the Dragon Stone."

"Thanks," Rori said. "Drake is the one who spotted it."

"So, how did that Raven guy just vanish?" Ana asked.

"He used the red dust to get away," Griffith said. "But he will not get far. He is using borrowed magic. It is not very strong."

"I am glad the Dragon Stone is safe," said Bo. "And I know we can't give it to Emperor Song. But I do not know what to do. He will keep my family in prison if we do not give the stone to him." He looked like he was about to cry.

Then Drake saw something. Bo's Dragon Stone was glowing!

"Bo, look!" he said, pointing.

Bo looked down. His eyes grew wide. He was quiet for a moment. Then a huge grin spread across his face.

"It's happening!" he cried. "Shu is speaking to me — inside my head!"

GRIFFITH'S PLAN

Bo closed his eyes, listening to his dragon.

"What is Shu saying?" Rori whispered.

"That there is a dark cloud over the emperor," Bo said, opening his eyes. "A darkness that is not his own."

"Could it be Maldred?" Drake asked, thinking of the dark wizard.

Griffith nodded. "The dust the guard used looks like Maldred's dark magic. Maldred may be using the emperor to get to the dragons."

"Can Shu help?" Ana asked.

"She says that she can," Bo replied, "but that she needs to see the emperor in person." He looked at Griffith. "May I bring her to him?"

"I do not know all the secrets a Water Dragon holds," Griffith said. "If Shu says she can help, then I trust her."

"We should go to your kingdom right now, Bo!" Drake said. "I'll get Worm."

"Let us think this through, Drake," Griffith said. "I trust you and Bo to go on your own. I must stay here to protect the Dragon Stone. Ana and Rori can assist me. But we will need the help of my friend, Diego, too."

Griffith snapped his fingers. *POOF!* Drake jumped. A cloud of smoke filled the room. When it cleared, a short, fat wizard was standing there.

"Griffith! What's wrong?" Diego asked.

"Maldred is trying to steal the Dragon Stone," Griffith explained. "You and I must strengthen the charms that protect it."

Diego nodded. "I will do whatever you need, my friend."

Griffith turned to Bo and Drake. "Be careful. Let Shu try to remove the dark cloud from Emperor Song. Make sure Bo's family is safe. Then come right back."

"We will do our best," Bo said.

Drake had a scary thought. *I know Bo feels bad about trying to steal the Dragon Stone. But what if the emperor tells Bo to do something else? Like turn over our dragons? Would he do it to save his family?*

Drake wasn't sure what to think. But right now, he had to trust his friend.

"There is no time to waste!" said Griffith. "Drake, put a saddle on Worm."

"I'll be fast!" Drake promised, and he ran to Worm's cave.

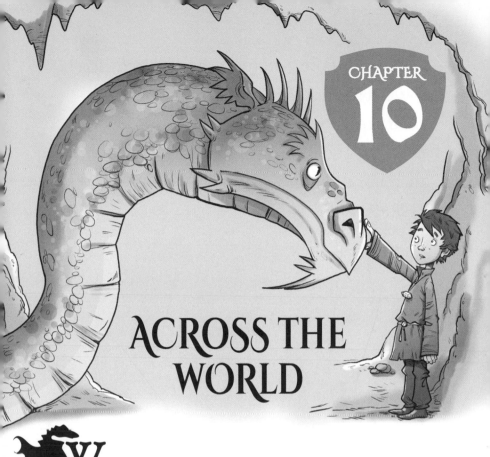

ACROSS THE WORLD

Worm, I need your help," Drake said. "We must go to the kingdom of Emperor Song. It might be dangerous, but we have to help the emperor and save Bo's family. Will you take us?"

Worm nodded. Drake quickly put his saddle on him. Then Bo rushed into the cave, riding Shu.

"Now, Drake, we just touch Worm for his power to work. Right?" Bo asked.

Drake nodded.

Bo touched Worm, and Shu touched Worm with her tail.

"Ready!" Bo said.

Drake took a deep breath. "Okay, Worm. Please take us to the kingdom of Emperor Song."

Worm's body started to glow. Green light filled the room. It grew brighter and brighter. Drake's heart raced.

The green light exploded. Drake felt weird. His stomach flip-flopped.

Then the light faded. He blinked. A moon shone in the sky above.

"We are here," said Bo.

"You did it, Worm!" Drake cheered.

He looked around. It was nighttime in the kingdom. A towering building rose up in front of them. Moonlight shone on a big, round pond in front of the building. Cherry trees lined the walkway around the pond.

Drake and Bo climbed down from their dragons.

"That is Emperor Song's palace," Bo said.

"We must bring Shu to him right away," Drake said.

"Yes. But he will be angry when he sees that I do not have the Dragon Stone," Bo said.

Drake shook his head. "I still don't get it, Bo," he said. "Why didn't you tell me what the feather meant? And about the note?"

"The note said not to tell anybody," Bo replied.

The boys walked away from the dragons as they talked.

"But I'm not anybody. I'm your *friend*," Drake shot back.

"Drake, I am sorry. I —" Bo stopped. A rustling sound came from the trees. "What was that?"

Drake looked up. He saw something move in the treetops. He held his breath.

"The Raven Guards!" Bo whispered.

Four guards dressed in black swooped down.

"Worm! Shu! Help us!" Drake yelled.

A dozen more guards dropped down around Worm and Shu.

Before the dragons could act, the Raven Guards carried Drake and Bo away with magical speed.

EMPEROR SONG

Drake struggled as a Raven Guard held him under one arm.

"It is no use," Bo whispered. "They are much stronger than we are. We cannot fight them. And they are taking us to Emperor Song, which is what we want."

"But we need Shu!" Drake whispered back. "Do you think our dragons escaped those other guards?"

Bo frowned. "They may have been captured. We will have to face the emperor without them."

Drake looked down at his Dragon Stone.

Worm, give me a message.

But the stone didn't glow. Then Drake thought of something. *Emperor Song might see our pieces of the stone! What if he tries to take them?*

"Quick!" he whispered to Bo. "Hide your Dragon Stone."

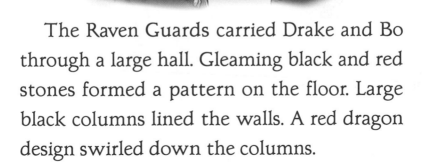

The Raven Guards carried Drake and Bo through a large hall. Gleaming black and red stones formed a pattern on the floor. Large black columns lined the walls. A red dragon design swirled down the columns.

The guards took them to a large room. A dozen more Raven Guards waited for them there.

A man in a red robe sat on a white throne. He had a long mustache, a pointy black beard, and wore a black hat. A thin smile spread across his face when he saw Bo. It reminded Drake of a field snake's smile.

Bo whispered to Drake. "See the evil in his eyes? This is not the emperor I remember."

The guards let go of the boys and pushed them toward the emperor.

"Bo," Emperor Song said, "I am surprised that you came so quickly. Where is my Dragon Stone?"

Bo looked at Drake, panicked. They had been counting on Shu to help them deal with the emperor. Without Shu, they had no plan. And without Worm, there was no way out.

"Well, Bo?" the emperor asked. "I am waiting."

"I . . . I don't have the Dragon Stone, Emperor," Bo said in a small voice.

A dark look came over the emperor's face. "No Dragon Stone?! Then you have failed me!"

"It's not Bo's fault!" Drake blurted out.

Emperor Song looked down at Drake. "A child dares to speak to the emperor this way?! Take them to the prison! These boys shall join Bo's family."

Drake squeezed his eyes shut. *Worm? Worm? Can you hear me, Worm? We need help!*

"Take them away!" Emperor Song yelled. Then the doors burst open.

Swoooooooooooosh! A giant wave of water flooded the room!

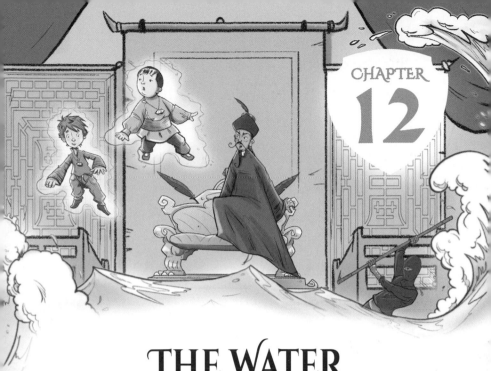

THE WATER DRAGON'S POWER

he emperor jumped onto the seat of his throne. The strong wave knocked the guards off their feet. Drake held his breath, waiting to be knocked down, too. Then his whole body began to tingle. He looked down.

He was floating above the water! *But how?*

"It's the dragons!" Bo called out. Drake turned and saw that Bo was floating in midair, too. "Shu must have used the water from the pond to break into the castle. And Worm is keeping us above the water!"

Shu floated into the room, traveling on top of the waves. Her blue scales shimmered. Her eyes gleamed. Worm came behind her. As he slid across the floor, the water moved away from him.

Shu floated over to Bo. He climbed on her and gripped her saddle. Worm slid underneath Drake. Drake felt Worm's hold leave him, and he dropped right onto his dragon's saddle.

Emperor Song pointed at the two dragons. "Guards! Grab them!" he cried. But his Raven Guards were woozy after being hit by the wave. They slowly got to their feet, splashing in the knee-high water.

"More guards will come!" the emperor said. "You cannot harm me. I am the emperor! I am the ruler of this kingdom! Get back!"

Then Shu glided
right up to the
emperor. Her huge
head stopped just
inches away from
his.

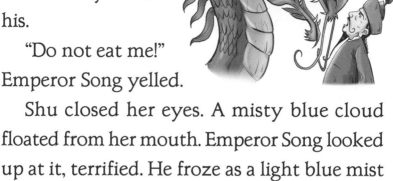

"Do not eat me!"
Emperor Song yelled.

Shu closed her eyes. A misty blue cloud
floated from her mouth. Emperor Song looked
up at it, terrified. He froze as a light blue mist
rained down on his head.

The look on his face changed. He looked
peaceful.

"What a beautiful creature," the emperor said, reaching out. He gently touched Shu's nose.

Back on their feet, the Raven Guards charged toward Shu.

"STOP!" Emperor Song called out. "Our guests must not be harmed!"

Drake and Bo looked at each other.

"Guests?" Drake mouthed to Bo. It seemed like Shu's powers were working!

Emperor Song stood up. "I am sorry, Bo," he said. "I do not know what came over me. I should never have asked you to steal the Dragon Stone. I fear I was under a dark spell. But your dragon ... your dragon has somehow saved me."

Bo's Dragon Stone began to glow beneath his shirt. Bo closed his eyes. After a minute, he opened them. "Shu has a very special, secret power. She can wash away any spell. She has just broken the spell that Maldred placed on you."

"I should never have let that wizard into the palace," said the emperor. "Maldred's dark spell made me force you to steal the Dragon Stone. My Raven Guards were only obeying my orders."

"Does this mean Bo's family will be safe?" Drake asked.

"Of course," Emperor Song said. "I will release them from prison."

Bo bowed his head. "Thank you, Emperor."

Drake smiled. He was happy for Bo.

Then, without warning, he heard Worm's voice in his head.

Danger is coming!

Drake looked up. A swarm of glowing red balls flew into the throne room. They came at them at lightning speed!

"It's Maldred's dark magic! Get down!" Drake yelled.

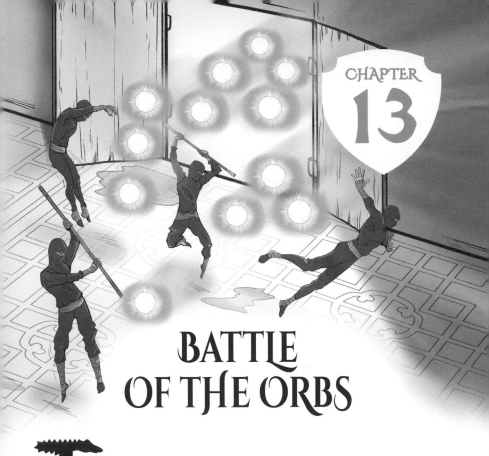

BATTLE
OF THE ORBS

The red balls of light darted around the room like angry bees.

Zap! One of the orbs shot a beam of dark energy at a Raven Guard. It knocked down the guard.

One of the orbs zoomed right at Drake. Worm's eyes glowed.

Boom! The orb exploded.

Another red ball zoomed toward Bo. *Bam!* The orb burst. Worm had used the power of his mind to destroy them.

Blast! Shu tried hitting one of the glowing balls with a jet of water. But the water bounced off it.

Around them, the Raven Guards were jumping and dodging. One swung a fighting stick at an orb. But like Shu's water, it didn't harm it at all.

Suddenly, the orbs grouped together. They zoomed all at once toward the dragons. Drake gripped Worm's saddle.

Boom! Boom! Boom! Worm blasted them with his green light, and they exploded.

Then the room became quiet. Drake looked around. Worm had destroyed all of the orbs!

"Good job, Worm," he said, patting Worm's neck.

Emperor Song stepped forward.

"You and your dragons have saved us again," he said. "I thank you. And Bo, I will tell your family of your bravery here today."

"Thank you, Emperor. Now I must return to Bracken. The dragons need me," said Bo. "But please tell my family that I will try to come see them soon."

"I will," said the emperor. "And I am sorry for what I have put them through. I will make it up to them."

Bo thanked the emperor. He and Shu both touched Worm.

"Good-bye, Bo," said the emperor. "You have made your kingdom proud."

"Let's go home, Worm," Drake said. They left Emperor Song's kingdom behind them in a flash of green light.

RISE AGAINST MALDRED

econds later, Drake and Bo landed in the Training Room. Rori and Ana rushed over.

"You're okay!" Ana cried.

The boys climbed down from their dragons.

"Yes!" replied Bo. "My family is safe and the emperor is no longer under Maldred's dark spell."

"Shu and Worm were amazing!" Drake said. "You should have seen them in action!"

Then Drake noticed the worried look on the girls' faces. "What's wrong?"

"Something has happened to Diego," Rori said. "Come see."

Drake and Bo followed the girls to Griffith's workshop. Griffith leaned over Diego, who was stretched out on a cot.

"Is he asleep?" Drake asked.

"Not exactly," said Griffith. "Diego tried out a new spell — to find Maldred. But it put him into a deep sleep. He has been like this for hours. I am very worried."

Drake and Bo looked at each other.

"Griffith!" cried Bo. "I think we can help. Shu broke the spell that Maldred put on Emperor Song. She has the power to undo magic spells."

Griffith clapped his hands together. "What a wonderful secret power! It may be just what we need to break Diego's spell, too! Can you please ask her to help him?"

Bo nodded and turned to Shu. "Please wash away the spell that is on Diego."

Shu glided right up to Diego. Another misty, blue cloud floated from her mouth. It rained down on Diego. Then he opened his eyes.

"Dragon!" he yelled, sitting up.

"Don't be scared, Diego," said Griffith. "It is only Shu."

"Not Shu," said Diego. "I saw another dragon as I slept."

"What did you see exactly?" Griffith asked Diego.

"Maldred! He had a dragon — an evil dragon with four heads!" Diego said.

"But dragons aren't evil. Are they?" Ana asked.

"Not by nature. But when in the hands of Maldred . . ." Griffith's voice trailed off.

"We should do something," Rori said.

"Yes!" agreed Ana. "We need to find Maldred before he and this four-headed dragon attack the kingdom!"

"Maldred attacked us in Emperor Song's throne room," said Drake. "He sent more red orbs. Lots of them."

"But Worm blasted them all!" added Bo.

Griffith stroked his beard.

"Dragon Masters, you are right," he said. "We cannot risk waiting for Maldred to attack again. We must find him and stop him before it's too late."

"All of us?" Drake asked. "And our dragons, too?"

Griffith nodded. "Yes."

Drake looked at his friends and smiled.

Together, we can face anything! Drake thought.

Griffith turned to the Dragon Masters. "Now, then. It is time for us all to rise against Maldred!"

TRACEY WEST loves the ocean. Ever since she can remember, Tracey has gone on a trip to the shore each year with her family. The ocean reminds her of Shu the Water Dragon. They are both powerful and peaceful at the same time.

Tracey has written dozens of books for kids. She does her writing in the house she shares with her husband and three stepkids. She also has plenty of animal friends to keep her company. She has two dogs, seven chickens, and one cat, who sits on her desk when she writes! Thankfully, the cat does not weigh as much as a dragon.

GRAHAM HOWELLS lives with his wife and two sons in west Wales, a place full of castles, and legends of wizards and dragons.

There are many stories about the dragons of Wales. One story tells of a large, legless dragon—sort of like Worm! Graham's home is also near where Merlin the great wizard is said to lie asleep in a crystal cave.

Graham has illustrated several books. He has created artwork for film, television, and board games, too. Graham also writes stories for children. In 2009, he won the Tir Na N'Og award for *Merlin's Magical Creatures*.

DRAGON MASTERS
SECRET OF THE WATER DRAGON

Questions and Activities

Look back at the words and pictures to find **CLUES** that something was bothering Bo.

Why does someone want to steal the Dragon Stone?

Look back at the words and pictures to **DESCRIBE** the Raven Guards.

What is Shu the Water Dragon's secret power?

Write a story about what might have happened in Diego's dream.